FAR OUT

CLASSIC STORIES

INTRODUCING...

YOLANDA

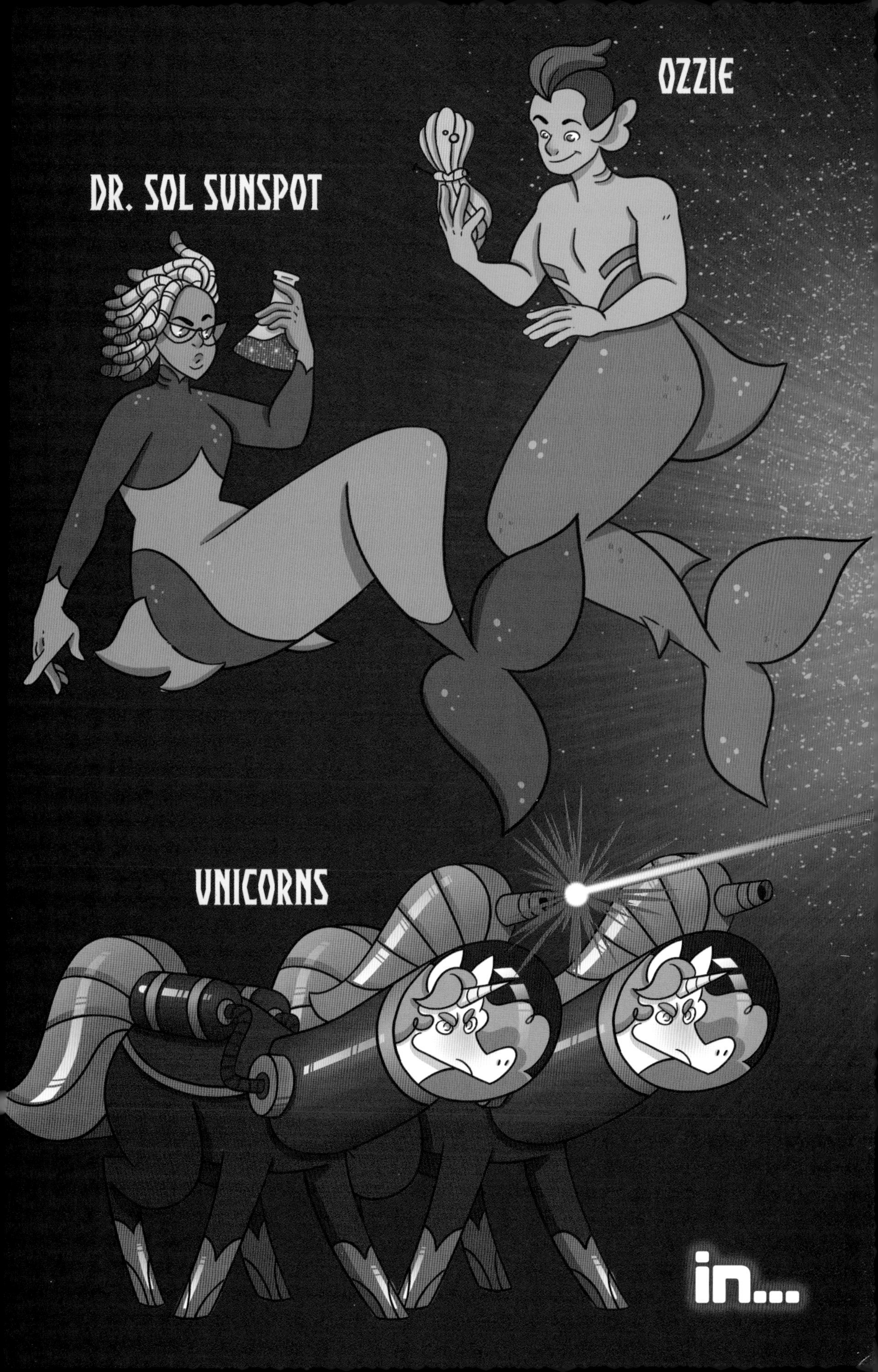

OZZIE

DR. SOL SUNSPOT

UNICORNS

in...

Far Out Classic Stories are
published by Stone Arch Books,
an imprint of Capstone.
1710 Roe Crest Drive
North Mankato, Minnesota 56003
capstonepub.com

Copyright © 2022 by Capstone.
All rights reserved. No part of this publication may be reproduced in whole or in part, or stored in a retrieval system, or transmitted in any form or by any means, electronic, mechanical, photocopying, recording, or otherwise, without written permission of the publisher.

Library of Congress Cataloging-in-Publication Data
Title: War of the worlds–Unicorns vs. Mermaids : a graphic novel / by Benjamin Harper ; illustrated by Jimena S. Sarquiz.
Other titles: Unicorns vs. Mermaids
Description: North Mankato, Minnesota : Stone Arch Books, an imprint of Capstone, [2022] I Series: Far out classic stories I Audience: Ages 8-11. I Audience: Grades 4-6. I Summary: In this graphic novel loosely based on H.G. Wells's *The War of the Worlds*, armed unicorns in a huge spaceship invade the peaceful mermaid planet of Ocea.
Identifiers: LCCN 2021029809 (print) I LCCN 2021029810 (ebook) I ISBN 9781663977106 (hardcover) I ISBN 9781666330281 (paperback) I ISBN 9781666330298 (pdf) I ISBN 9781666330311 (kindle edition)
Subjects: LCSH: Mermaids–Comic books, strips, etc. I Mermaids–Juvenile fiction. I Unicorns–Comic books, strips, etc. I Unicorns–Juvenile Fiction. I Extrasolar planets–Comic books, strips, etc. I Extrasolar planets–Juvenile fiction. I Graphic novels. I Science fiction. I CYAC: Graphic novels. I Science fiction. I Mermaids–Fiction. I Unicorns–Fiction. I Extrasolar planets–Fiction. I LCGFT: Graphic novels. I Science fiction.
Classification: LCC PZ7.7.H366 War 2022 (print) I LCC PZ7.7.H366 (ebook) I DDC 741.5/973–dc23
LC record available at https://lccn.loc.gov/2021029809
LC ebook record available at https://lccn.loc.gov/2021029810

Designed by Hilary Wacholz
Edited by Mandy Robbins
Lettered by Jaymes Reed

Printed and bound in China. PO4971

FAR OUT CLASSIC STORIES

WAR OF THE WORLDS
UNICORNS VS. MERMAIDS

A GRAPHIC NOVEL

BY BENJAMIN HARPER
ILLUSTRATED BY JIMENA S. SARQUIZ

Welcome to the planet Ocea, a world completely covered in water.
WATERVILLE
Near the town of Waterville, the citizens were tending to their annual kelp harvest.

This year's kelp crop is looking really great!
I can't wait to start making kelp cakes again.

FWOOM!
What was *that*?!
Come on—let's go look!

What could it be?
I hope it's not dangerous!

It's . . . it's beautiful!

But where did it come from?
And what does it want?

Dr. Sol Sunspot was planet Ocea's leading scientist. She and her assistant, Ozzie, had arrived to study the phenomenon.

Greetings! We mean you *no harm.*

What's happening?
I don't know. Be ready for anything.

BZZT
GULP!

They're not here to make friends . . .

Everybody swim! Get out of here!
HELP!
SWIM!!!
AAAAH!

I got a piece of debris from the ship. Let's take it back to my lab!
Come on, Yolanda! Let's follow the experts.

What should we do?
This is unlike anything we've ever seen before! I need more information.
I'm Yolanda, and she's Kiki. We want to help!
You two can stick with us. I'm Ozzie, and she's Sol—er Dr. Sunspot.

WWT! WWWWT!
Oh no . . .
I'm afraid to look!

It's what I feared—an invasion!
We are totally unprepared for this!

Help!!!
They've got me!

We must do something!
They'll take over the whole planet!

The four panicked merpeople swam away from the chaos as fast as they could!
SWOOSH!

We've got to contact Ocea Government Headquarters!
WATERVILLE
Let's get back to Waterville!

But when they got to town . . .
Oh no!
I don't believe it!

ZZZT!
RIING!
Help!
Save me!

What are we going to do?
We need to stay hidden!

They're capturing everybody!
They're not getting us!

If we make it into that sewer grate, we'll be safer below the street.

Ozzie's right. And we can follow the sewer line back to my lab!
Ok, on the count of three. One . . . two . . .

THREE!
SNAP
We're safe.
But what's going on everywhere else?

EVERYWHERE ELSE.

Merpeople fled their homes looking for safety.
But no matter where they went, the unicorns were there.
Meanwhile, back in Waterville . . .
We're almost to my lab. Maybe we can figure out how to defeat these intruders by analyzing the debris I found.

Quick! Let's get inside!
DR. SOL
STARFISH LABS.
And fast! I hear something coming!

Let's see what's on the news. Maybe someone knows what's going on.
While you watch that, I'll analyze what this metal is made of.

Breaking news, reporting live from the news station bunker. The planet has been taken over by alien invaders!

This metal appears to have no weakness. I don't see how we can break through it.

Our troops have tried to fight against the alien unicorns, but nothing seems to stop them.
No weapons can penetrate their armor.

Officials have issued this statement:

Do not go out in public. Find a safe place to hide—and stay there!

We may not be safe here. They could find us.
We need to find a safe place where we can try to figure out how to defeat the invaders.
I think I know a place!

We're almost there.
I hope it's safe.
If not, we're in trouble.

There it is!
The Old Sea King's Castle!

The coast is clear.
Quick, inside!

They searched for a safe place to hide inside the castle.
It doesn't look like they've been here.
Maybe they thought it looked deserted.
Let's find a good hiding spot.

I have a hunch about those unicorns' helmets.
Why are they all wearing them?
Maybe they need them to survive.
Exactly right, Ozzie!

But to prove my theory, we have to get close to one. That could prove deadly. We'll need weapons.

But suddenly . . .
CRRUNCH!
Oh no!
We've been discovered!

The group hid and stayed perfectly still.

An hour later . . .

Do you think they're gone?
I haven't seen any light for a while!
One of us should go see!

No! We stay put until we can figure out how to stop these monsters!

Well I can't stay in here anymore– I'm going to look!

Suddenly . . .
What was that!?!

Aliens! What is that cylinder on the side of the metal armor? Some kind of weapon?

The alien unicorns were searching for merpeople to take prisoner.

They've launched a probe to look for us!
If they discover us, we're goners!

The probe continued its search.

When that probe comes over here I'm going to smash it with this rock.
And when I do, you all need to flip this bed over and swim away from them as fast as you can!
It was now or never for the merpeople!
GO!

FWOOSH!

After their escape . . .
That was so strange.
Don't you mean terrifying?
Oh yeah, their gills were covered up!
No, I mean strange. How do they breathe in those suits?
Maybe they don't breathe with gills?

They swam away as fast as they could and kept on going until . . .
WATERVILLE
Look! Merpeople are returning to Waterville!
How is it safe?

Refugee Camp
Merpeople Welcome
Why is everyone coming back here?
The battle must have moved away from the city.
The governments of the world are going to use untested prototype Aqua-weaponry against the aliens.
We are getting live footage.
If this doesn't work, we have no other way to fight these invaders. We will have to surrender.

Troops are launching the attack now!
I hope this works.
If it doesn't, we're in even bigger trouble.

Troops are using sonic water blasts to try to crack these ships open.

After several minutes, it appears these weapons have no effect on the alien ships.

I'm afraid that was our last hope.
Oh no! What are we going to do?
We'll have to test our theory. We'll need weapons.

Suddenly . . .

Merpeople! This is OUR PLANET!
And we must defend it!
Grab whatever you can and fight!

The final battle for planet Ocea had begun!

Watch out for their horns!
FOR OCEA!

Noooo!
Yolanda, get behind me!
BZZT

Go back to your own planet and leave us alone!

BOOM!

HELP!

All appeared to be lost. The unicorns were triumphant.
We surrender!
CRAAACK!
Take this!

Glug glug bluggrgllhhhhh!
AHA!
FWOOM!
Without realizing it, Kiki had proven Sol's theory about the unicorns' weakness!

Everyone! Grab what you can and smash their helmets!
We can still win this thing!
Yolanda was right! They don't breathe through gills. They use their mouths!
EVERYONE! CRACK THEIR HELMETS!

The tide of battle had finally turned.

Spread the word!
Crack their helmets and we will win the war!

Attention all citizens! Break the unicorns' helmets with whatever you can!
They can't breathe underwater!

Keep it up! They are retreating!
HOORAY!!!
GULP!
The unicorns had lost!

But now the citizens of Ocea had to pick up the pieces.
Are you ok?
Yes, thank you for helping me!
They would have to rebuild their cities . . .

. . . and replant their crops.

But together, they knew they could get through hard times!
We did it!
I'm glad you're all ok!

They even planned to improve their society because of the attack . . .
The unicorns have technology that far surpasses ours.

LEAVE A little SPARKLE wherever YOU GO
And we are studying it to see if it can be used for purposes other than war.
The possibilities are endless!

We are hoping we'll be able to use what we discover to help us rebuild Ocea!

Do you think the unicorns will ever attack again?
A very good question!

The unicorns can't survive on our world without their oxygen tanks.
They didn't count on us figuring that out!
Our beautiful ocean world saved us from their attack.

And if they ever come back . . . we'll be READY.

OCEA FOREVER
HOOORAY!!!

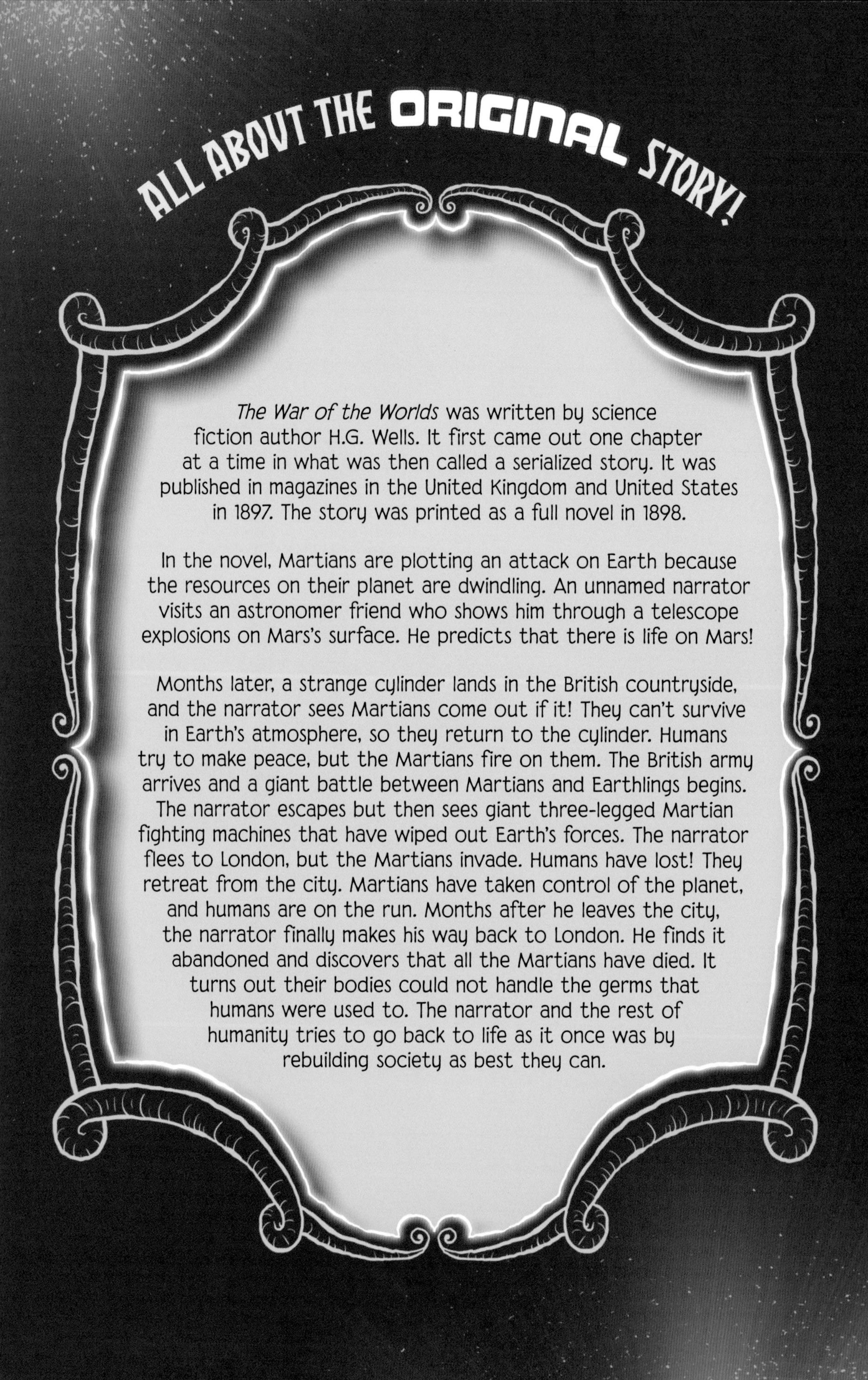

ALL ABOUT THE ORIGINAL STORY!

The War of the Worlds was written by science fiction author H.G. Wells. It first came out one chapter at a time in what was then called a serialized story. It was published in magazines in the United Kingdom and United States in 1897. The story was printed as a full novel in 1898.

In the novel, Martians are plotting an attack on Earth because the resources on their planet are dwindling. An unnamed narrator visits an astronomer friend who shows him through a telescope explosions on Mars's surface. He predicts that there is life on Mars!

Months later, a strange cylinder lands in the British countryside, and the narrator sees Martians come out if it! They can't survive in Earth's atmosphere, so they return to the cylinder. Humans try to make peace, but the Martians fire on them. The British army arrives and a giant battle between Martians and Earthlings begins. The narrator escapes but then sees giant three-legged Martian fighting machines that have wiped out Earth's forces. The narrator flees to London, but the Martians invade. Humans have lost! They retreat from the city. Martians have taken control of the planet, and humans are on the run. Months after he leaves the city, the narrator finally makes his way back to London. He finds it abandoned and discovers that all the Martians have died. It turns out their bodies could not handle the germs that humans were used to. The narrator and the rest of humanity tries to go back to life as it once was by rebuilding society as best they can.

A FAR OUT GUIDE TO THE STORY'S ACTION-PACKED TWISTS

In the original book, it's humans vs. Martians, not merpeople vs. unicorns!

The Martians die due to germs on Earth. Unicorns flee Ocea because they can't breathe underwater!

Martians arrive on Earth in cylinders. Unicorns travel to Ocea in giant metallic unicorn ships.

In the original story, human technology is useless against the Martians. On Ocea, the merpeople fight back and figure out how to win!

VISUAL QUESTIONS

In graphic novels, illustrators have different ways of showing action. How can you tell that something is moving quickly through the water? What hints does the illustrator give?

Who is speaking in this word balloon on page 17? How do you know? For hints, go back and look in the surrounding panels.

What clues did the illustrator give to show that Yolanda is whispering in this panel? Why do you think she is whispering?

Comics aren't always drawn realistically. The illustrator exaggerated many of the characters' expressions. What do you think of this choice? How does it affect the story's tone? Find at least two other examples of over-the-top expressions in the book.

Kiki has just realized something. What is it, and why is it important to the story? Try writing a thought bubble that shows what's going through her mind.

AUTHOR

Benjamin Harper has worked as an editor at DC Comics and Lucasfilm Ltd. He currently lives in Los Angeles, where he writes, watches monster movies, and hangs out with his cats Marjorie and Jerry, a betta fish named Toby, four newts, and a bog garden full of carnivorous plants. His other books include the Bug Girl series, *Obsessed With Star Wars, Rolling with BB-8, Hansel & Gretel & Zombies*, and many more.

ILLUSTRATOR

Jimena S. Sarquiz was born in Mexico City, Mexico. She studied illustration at the Escuela Nacional de Artes Plásticas (National School of Plastic Arts) and has since worked and lived in the United States as well as Spain. Jimena now lives in Mexico City again, working as an illustrator and comic book artist. Her art has appeared in many children's books and magazines.

GLOSSARY

alien (AY-lee-uhn)—a creature from a different planet—perhaps a laser-shooting unicorn

gill (GIL)—a body part on the side of fish and merpeople used to breathe underwater

kelp (KELP)—large, brown seaweed, the main ingredient in kelp cakes

native (NAY-tuhv)—belonging to one's original surroundings

phenomenon (fe-NOM-uh-non)—something very unusual or remarkable, perhaps a unicorn spaceship

probe (PROHB)—a small spacecraft sent to gather data and find terrified merpeople

prototype (PROH-tuh-tipe)—the first version of an invention that tests an idea to see if it will work

sewer grate (SOO-ur GRAYT)—a grid of metal bars that leads to a system of pipes that carries away liquid and solid waste

OLD FAVORITES. NEW SPINS.

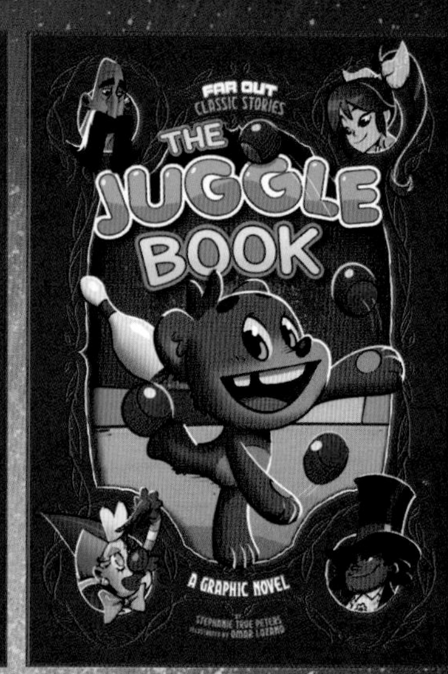

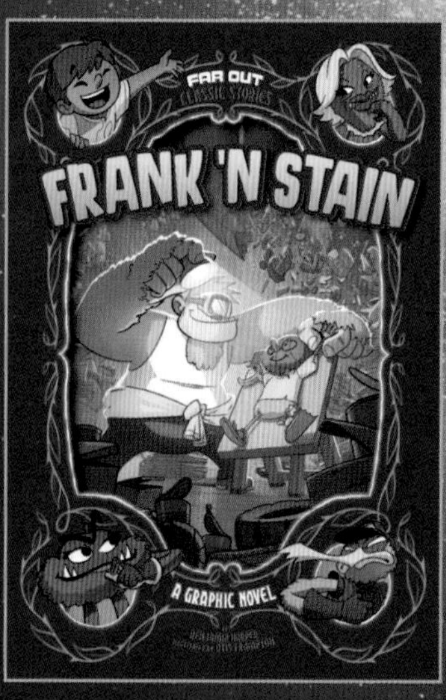

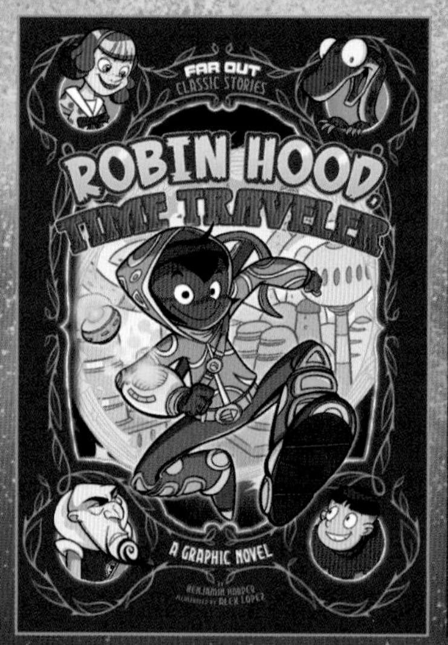

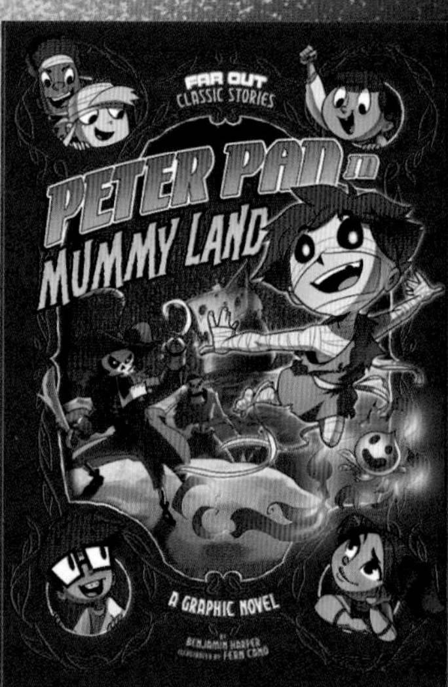

FAR OUT CLASSIC STORIES

ONLY FROM CAPSTONE!